Guildtown Primary School
School Road
Guildtown
Perthshire PH2 6BX
Tel. 0821 640382

01469

Text copyright © Jamie Rix 1999
Illustrations copyright © Ross Collins 1999

First published in Great Britain in 1999
by Macdonald Young Books
an imprint of Wayland Publishers Ltd
61 Western Road
Hove
East Sussex
BN3 1JD

Find Macdonald Young Books on the internet at
http://www.myb.co.uk

The right of Jamie Rix to be identified as the author
and Ross Collins the illustrator of this Work has been asserted
by them in accordance with the Copyright, Designs and
Patents Act 1988.

Designed and Typeset by Backup Creative Services, Dorset DT10 1DB
Printed in Hong Kong

British Library Cataloguing in Publication Data available

ISBN: 0 7500 2696 0

JAMIE RIX

The Vile Smile

Illustrated by Ross Collins

MACDONALD YOUNG BOOKS

Chapter One

There once was a bad-tempered princess called Viola. Her subjects called her Princess Vile. She was a spoilt little brat, a stamper and a screamer who always got her own way. This was because she had the prettiest smile in the world. She could charm the birds out of the trees with a flash of her gleaming white teeth.

One day, she met Prince Moneybags, the heir to the neighbouring throne. He was handsome, in a chunky sort of way, and the princess decided that she would marry him. Her father, the king, was delighted.

Prince Moneybags was extremely rich and his money would buy the king that speedboat he'd always wanted.

But nobody thought to ask Prince Moneybags if he wanted to marry Princess Vile. And he didn't. He hated her tantrums and thought she needed a good telling-off.

But when the princess tossed him a smile, he was captivated by its beauty.

Reason flew out of the window and Prince Moneybags fell under her spell. The marriage was the talk of both kingdoms, and the king was the happiest man alive. At last he could learn how to waterski.

Then, one summer's day, an accident changed the course of history. Whilst shooting rabbits in a cornfield, Princess Vile tripped on a servant, tumbled over, and lost her diamond engagement ring down a rabbit hole. But that was not all that she'd lost.

She was in such a foul temper when she returned to the palace that her mother locked up the royal china for fear that the princess would smash it to pieces. Princess Vile lay on her bed with a face like an old boot and screamed and wailed and spat and hollered and kicked her little legs in the air like a three-year-old child.

When Prince Moneybags saw her surly, unsmiling face, he fell out of love with her and called the wedding off.

"Why?" boomed the shocked king.

"The princess has lost her smile," said Prince Moneybags.

"Well, where has it gone?" wept the queen, who had already bought her dress for the wedding.

"Not my problem," said the prince, as
he rode off into the sunset and left the
king in a bit of pickle.

"We must find the smile immediately!"
the king roared. "Viola must marry this
prince or I shall never get my speedboat."

The courtiers rushed through the palace turning mattresses, emptying cupboards, tilting thrones and lifting carpets, but no matter how hard they searched, they could not find it.

Princess Vile's charming smile had vanished into thin air.

Either that or it had fallen down the rabbit hole with her diamond ring. But nobody thought to look.

Chapter Two

The king did not like the look of his daughter's new face. It was sullen and sulky and it frightened the royal cats and dogs.

"It must have been stolen!" he bellowed.
"I don't care what it takes, find me the
person who stole the smile and bring them
to the palace."

People with smiles on their faces were plucked off the streets by armed guards and dragged into the palace, where they were tied roughly to a chair and made to prove that their smile was their own.

The princess sat facing them on her throne watching each of them smile in turn, then shaking her head.

"Too toothy," she said. "Too gappy, too sneery, too creepy, too weasly, too beamy, too leery, and much too much lipstick. My smile was much prettier than all of these."

The news that smiling people were being arrested and tied roughly to chairs spread throughout the kingdom. People were terrified. Within a week nobody smiled anymore. The kingdom became a land of gloom and doom. Smiles became a thing of the past.

The king was being fitted for his waterskiing wetsuit, when the First Minister broke the news.

"Your Majesty," he quaked, "I regret to tell you that the princess's smile has gone forever. We cannot find it."

The king was furious.

"Have you searched everywhere?" he thundered.

"Everywhere," trembled the First Minister.

"The highest peak, the deepest ocean, the darkest cave?" the king quizzed.

"Even the muckiest sewer," grimaced the First Minister.

"And the Village of the Glums?" pressed the king.

The First Minister hesitated.

"But nobody smiles in the Village of the Glums," he faltered. "That's why it's called the Village of the Glums."

"Search it!" boomed the king.

Chapter Three

The armed guards were dispatched to the
Village of the Glums, where, lo and
behold, they found a young man called
Reg, a simple, ugly lad, sitting in a field
talking to a rabbit. Unfortunately for him,
he was smiling.

Reg was tied roughly to a chair and dragged into the throne room to face the bad-tempered Princess Vile. He told his story honestly. He told her how he had stumbled on a smiling rabbit that had caught its tail in a tangled blackberry bush.

He told her how the rabbit had given him its smile in exchange for setting it free. He told her how his new smile had made him the happiest man in the world, because his childhood sweetheart had been captivated by its beauty. She had fallen under its spell and agreed to be his wife.

But as he told his story he made the mistake of smiling at the princess. He charmed the birds out of the trees with a flash of his gleaming white teeth, and she fell under the smile's spell.

"He's beautiful," she swooned. "I'm in love."

"So am I," grinned Reg. "With Gloria."

Princess Vile stamped her sulky foot on the ground and threw a temper tantrum.

"I want my magic smile back to make you love me!" she bellowed. "Bring me that smile." And before Reg could move, the guards had wiped the smile off his face with a dishcloth and had handed it the princess.

She quickly slipped it on and smiled at Reg with a smile that charmed the birds out of the trees. She opened her mouth and flashed her gleaming white teeth.

"Now, will you be my husband?" she beamed. The spoilt princess waited for him to fall under the smile's spell, to swoon at her feet and give her his heart, but Reg was unmoved.

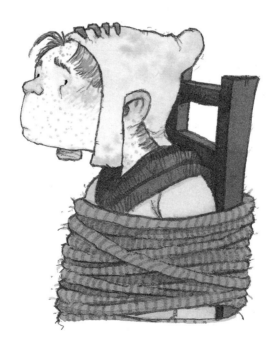

"I can't," he said. "For all your pretty smile, Princess Viola, I don't love you. I'm already engaged to be married."

"Then dump her!" snapped the princess as her smile started to crack. "She can't possibly be as pretty as me."

"You will do no such thing!" fumed the king who'd just come in from his waterskiing class. "This boy is a thief. Take him outside, pelt him with rotten tomatoes, then banish him from my kingdom!"

While Reg was led away to be pelted, the king put his foot down. "You're going to marry Prince Speedboat... I mean Moneybags!" he declared.

"No I'm not!" screamed the princess, tearing the smile off her face. "Give me what I want or I'll throw this smile out of the window."

"But Viola," protested the king, "if you do that Prince Moneybags will never marry you!"

"Good!" she sneered. "I don't want Moneybags, I want Reg!"

The king tried to be firm.

"Your king has spoken," he said weakly, then rather wished he hadn't, because the spiteful princess was true to her word and hurled the smile out of the window.

She watched it as it floated down the palace wall and landed in the cart that was taking Reg into town to be pelted.

Chapter Four

As you know, the bad-tempered princess
always got what she wanted. That night
she climbed over the balcony and slid
down the trailing ivy outside her bedroom.

She ran through the kingdom and found
Reg in a cow shed. He was covered in
tomatoes and holding hands with a glum
girl who had a face like a doughnut.

"Who are you?" the princess snapped
crossly.

"I'm Gloria," said the girl. "I'm his childhood sweetheart."

"Well push off," said the rude princess. "Reg is mine."

"I'm afraid not," said Reg. "Gloria and I are to be married today."

"But you can't marry her!" ranted the livid Princess Vile. "She's ugly."

"Not to me," said Reg. The princess stamped her foot and screamed and screamed until she was blue in the face.

"Then give me back my smile, you thief!" she howled. "I need it to win back Prince Moneybags's heart." But for once, Princess Vile could not have what she wanted.

"I don't have it," said Reg.

"But I saw it land in your cart!" she screeched.

"He doesn't have it," said Gloria. The princess's ill-mannered shriek was so shrill that it curdled the cream in the milk churns.

"Well blow you both to billy-o!" she stropped. "I hate you once, I hate you twice, I hate you more times even than a plague of black boils!"

And with that, she turned on her heel, and in a fury, she stomped back to the palace, where the king and queen were rather sad to see her coming.

The horrible, sour-faced Princess Vile never did find her smile again. She stayed horrible and sour-faced for the rest of her life, and never got married.

Prince Moneybags wed a much nicer princess from an altogether happier kingdom, which meant that the greedy king never got his speedboat. He took up fly-fishing instead. His first catch was an old trout, which everyone agreed looked very much like his daughter.

After the foul-faced princess had left the
cow shed, Reg turned to his bride-to-be
and kissed her warty hand.

"I love you, Gloria," he said with simple
honesty.

"And I love you, Reg," she replied. To
look at their glum faces you might have
thought that neither was happy, but you
would have been wrong. Deep in their
hearts they were smiling.

So was a certain torn-tailed rabbit, who was hopping through a cornfield with his twenty-three wives. On his face there was a smile, a right royal grin that charmed the birds out of the trees.

Look out for more titles in the Red Storybooks series:

Max and the Petnappers by Jeremy Strong

Max is alarmed to discover that his goldfish has been petnapped. But not as alarmed as when he meets Aunt Claribel – the very large, very loud and very famous opera singer. So famous that the petnappers, Belladonna Snitch and Gretel Grapple, decide she must be worth a lot more money than any pet. Luckily, Max is on their trail...

Frankie Stein's Robot by Roy Apps

Frankie Stein seems like an ordinary sort of lad. But he isn't. He's an inventor - that is, until Aunt Griselda comes to stay. She doesn't like his inventions. She insists that he spends all his spare time tidying up. Worst of all, she gives him huge, slurpy kisses. It's time for Frankie to invent something really spectacular - something that will leave Aunt Griselda speechless...

The Toad Prince by Linda Jennings

When Annie the servant girl finds a toad in the garden she wants to keep it as a pet. But the greedy Grindles, her employers, think the toad is really a prince under a spell...

The Disastrous Dog by Penelope Lively

When the Ropers bring a dog home from the animal sanctuary, they have no idea what they have let themselves in for. Soon the dog has the whole family running in circles round him.

You can buy all these books from your local bookseller, or they can be ordered direct from the publisher. For more information about Storybooks, write to: *The Sales Department, Macdonald Young Books, 61 Western Road, Hove, East Sussex BN3 1JD*